Cassette Ghosts

A Retro Horrors: The Lost Decade

Book meant to be read in no particular order.

Written By: B. Humphrey

Table of Contents

.... 1

Chapter 1: 3

Chapter 2: 9

Chapter 3: 15

Chapter 4: 21

Chapter 5: 27

Chapter 6: 33

Chapter 7: 39

Chapter 8: 45

Chapter 9: 51

Chapter 10: 57

Dedicated to you. May you always find a reason to smile.

Chapter 1:

The package arrived on a day when the sky pressed too close to the ground. Clouds, low and swollen like bruises, hung over the neighborhood, muting every sound beneath their suffocating weight. No cars passed on the street, no dogs barked from behind fences, and even the wind—usually restless this time of year—stayed unnervingly still.

At first, Biz thought the mailman had made a mistake. A small, worn-out envelope with **no return address** sat on the welcome mat in front of his door. It was the kind of yellowed paper you only saw in old libraries or thrift shops—edges brittle, curling inward, like it had been waiting years to be opened.

His name was scrawled on the front in red ink:

Brian "Biz" Humphrey.

No address. No stamps. Just his name, as if someone had placed it there by hand. Biz leaned closer, feeling the faint prickle of unease creeping up the back of his neck. Something about the envelope gave him the feeling you get in dreams—the kind where you know you shouldn't open a door, but your hand moves anyway.

He swiped it off the ground, fingers brushing the coarse paper. **It was cold.** Colder than the air around it, and it left a strange damp feeling on his fingertips, like it had been pulled out of some deep, dark place.

He stood frozen on the threshold, heart drumming lightly in his chest. The eerie quiet of the neighborhood pressed against his senses, and the faintest, most unsettling thought drifted into his mind: *Someone's watching.*

Biz closed the door behind him with a soft click, trying to shake the uneasy feeling. Inside the house, things felt just a little off—**like the furniture had shifted a half-inch in his absence,** or maybe the light bulbs were just a shade dimmer. His parents wouldn't be home until late, and the silence of the house wrapped around him too tightly, pressing against his skin.

He tore open the brittle envelope and pulled out the contents. Inside was a **cassette tape.** Black plastic with tiny, handwritten labels stuck to both sides. *SIDE A* was scrawled on one, and *SIDE B* on the other—no band names, no tracklist, nothing to suggest what was on it.

There was also a small, folded note tucked inside the envelope. Biz opened it carefully, trying not to tear the fragile paper. It read: **"Play me. Midnight. Alone."**

A chill slithered down his spine, and for a second, he thought he heard something—a faint whisper brushing the edge of his hearing, gone before he could focus on it. He looked around the room, the shadows seeming to thicken at the corners of his vision.

The living room felt too quiet. He could hear the refrigerator humming in the kitchen, the faint tick of the wall clock, and his own heartbeat drumming in his ears.

He turned the tape over in his hand, its weight strange and solid, as if it carried more than just music inside it. Something felt *wrong*—the way things feel when you find a door open that you're certain you locked.

That evening dragged like syrup on a cold day. Biz tried everything to pass the time—flipping through comic books, watching a half-busted VHS of *The Lost Boys*—but the thought of the cassette gnawed at him. It was like an itch he couldn't reach, a nagging weight at the back of his mind.

By the time 11:50 PM rolled around, the air in the house felt heavy, almost electric, like it did before a thunderstorm. Shadows stretched longer than they should have, and the faint hum of the refrigerator sounded a little too much like breathing.

Biz sat cross-legged on the floor of his room, the cassette player resting in front of him like a waiting predator. The plastic felt cool and slick in his hands as he slipped the tape into the player. His thumb hovered over the play button. **11:59 PM.**

Something moved at the edge of his vision—just a flicker in the corner of the room, a shadow slipping out of sight. He blinked, heart hammering, but there was nothing there when he turned to look.

And then, the clock hit midnight.

He pressed **Play.** The wheels inside the cassette player turned with a soft click, and at first, there was nothing—just the familiar hiss of blank tape spinning. But then, buried beneath the static, a voice emerged.

It wasn't music. It wasn't a song. It was a whisper.

Biz leaned closer, his skin prickling. The voice was faint, warped like it was being pulled from underwater. But as it grew clearer, his heart began to race. He recognized the voice. *"...Biz... it's me... Trevor..."* Biz's throat went dry. Trevor Langston—his next-door neighbor. His friend. Trevor had been missing for **three years.**

"Don't... don't trust the DJ..." Trevor's voice rasped through the speakers, crackling with interference. *"It's not over... they're still out there... and they're coming back..."*

The words sent a wave of cold through Biz's body, like a hand gripping the back of his neck. He stared at the cassette player, heart slamming against his ribs, every hair on his body standing on end. And then came **the sound.**

A low, haunting hum—just a note at first, vibrating deep and low, like the tuning of some strange instrument. The hum grew louder, filling the room with an eerie resonance that made his bones ache. Beneath it, Biz thought he heard other noises—a crackling fire, faint whispers, footsteps dragging through gravel. And then, **silence.**

The room felt colder. Biz glanced at the cassette player, heart still pounding, and reached for the Stop button. But before he could press it, the tape hissed again—and something new came through the speakers. A soft, rhythmic sound, like someone... **breathing.**

It wasn't Trevor this time. It was someone—or something—else. The breathing grew louder, closer, as if whoever was on the other end of the tape was standing right behind him.

Biz's hand shook as he reached for the Stop button, but just as his fingers brushed it, the breathing stopped. And then, a voice whispered from the tape, clear as day: *"We see you."* The lights in the room flickered. Biz gasped, stumbling backward, and the cassette player let out one final, sharp click as the tape stopped on its own.

The house plunged into a thick, unnatural silence. For a long moment, Biz sat frozen, heart thundering in his chest.

Then—slowly—he turned his head toward the doorway. The hallway beyond was dark. Too dark. And somewhere, deep within that darkness, he thought he saw a figure. Just a flicker—a shape standing still, watching him.

Biz slammed the Stop button and yanked the cassette from the player, his hands trembling. He stared at the tape, heart racing, trying to understand what he had just heard. Trevor's voice. Warnings. A low hum. And a whisper that still echoed in his mind: *"We see you."*

For a long time, Biz sat on the floor, gripping the tape so tightly his knuckles turned white. Something strange was happening—something he didn't understand. And somehow, the cassette was at the center of it.

He glanced at the clock on his nightstand. **12:07 AM.** The night stretched before him, silent and endless. And somewhere—out there in the dark—**something was waiting.**

Chapter 2:

Morning came sluggishly, as if the sun had to fight its way through thick curtains of fog. Biz had barely slept. He lay awake for hours, eyes locked on the cassette tape that now rested on his desk. It sat there like a dead thing, ordinary yet suffused with the weight of something unspeakable.

Every creak of the house had kept him on edge, every shadow seemed to shift when he wasn't looking. Even with the cassette out of the player, he swore he could still hear Trevor's voice echoing in his mind:

"They're still out there... don't trust the DJ..." The words clawed at him, leaving little room for thought or peace.

Finally, the morning light spilled weakly through his bedroom window, banishing the shadows—but not the unease. When he pulled on his hoodie and trudged downstairs for breakfast, the house felt too normal, **wrongly** normal, like nothing strange had ever happened. He knew better.

Biz biked to the park, his thoughts spiraling. The only person he could think to talk to about this—without sounding like a lunatic—was **Jace Lewis**. Jace was always up for weirdness. If anyone could make sense of this, it was his best friend.

Jace was already waiting by the skate ramp when Biz arrived, tearing through a bag of Cool Ranch Doritos with his usual chaotic energy. His ripped jeans and patched-up Clash t-shirt flapped slightly in the cool autumn breeze. "Biz!" Jace called, waving him over. "You look like you spent the night on Elm Street, man. What gives?"

Biz sat down beside him, heart still thudding with unease. He glanced around to make sure no one else was nearby before pulling the cassette from his pocket.

"This," Biz said, holding the tape between his fingers. "It showed up at my house last night." Jace arched an eyebrow. "A mysterious tape? Nice. Does it have, like, secret tracks from Led Zeppelin or something?" Biz shook his head. "It's... it's not music. It's messages. From Trevor." Jace's grin faltered. "Trevor? Langston? Dude—Trevor's been missing for years."

"I know," Biz whispered. He explained everything—the envelope, the weird note, and the tape's chilling contents. When he got to the part about the voice whispering, *"We see you,"* Jace's grin vanished entirely. "No way," Jace muttered, gripping the edge of the bench. "You're not messing with me?"

"Wish I was," Biz said, rubbing his eyes. "I thought I was dreaming at first, but... it was real, Jace. His voice was real."

They sat in silence for a moment, the wind picking up and scattering dead leaves around the skate ramp. Somewhere in the distance, the faint sound of Def Leppard played— the song Photograph drifting through the static.

Jace finally spoke. "Okay... let's say Trevor's voice really is on this thing. That means someone recorded him. Like... maybe right before he vanished." Biz nodded slowly. "Or maybe after." The words hung heavy between them. "You said something about a DJ?" Jace asked, squinting as he tried to piece things together. "What'd Trevor mean—'don't trust the DJ'?"

"I don't know." Biz ran a hand through his hair. "But he mentioned something else... about 'them still being out there.' It sounded like he was warning me."

"Okay. So, ghosts, cults, or weird conspiracy stuff—this is *definitely* our scene," Jace said, sitting up straighter. "We've gotta figure out what that DJ thing means. There's gotta be something to it."

Biz exhaled, relieved that his friend wasn't brushing him off. "You know that old radio station? 101.9 FM?" Jace's eyes lit up with recognition. "Dude, yeah! That was the creepy station everyone used to talk about. They shut it down before we even hit middle school. What was it called again? *The Final Hour*?"

Biz nodded. "Yeah. Trevor mentioned that, too. Something about the broadcast still being out there." Jace grinned, and there was a familiar gleam of excitement in his eyes—the kind of gleam that meant they were about to get into trouble. "Well, I say we check it out. Wanna meet Riley? He's down in his basement working on his new bass riffs."

Riley Moss lived just a few blocks away, in an old split-level house that smelled like motor oil and old pizza. His basement was their unofficial hangout—a cluttered, dimly lit space littered with amps, instruments, and posters of bands like Black Flag and The Misfits.

When they got there, **Riley** was slouched on the beat-up couch, strumming random notes on his bass guitar. He glanced up when Biz and Jace walked in, pushing his shaggy hair out of his eyes. "What's up, you degenerate rapscallions?" Riley greeted, smirking. Biz didn't waste time. He dropped the cassette on the table. "We found something. Something weird."

Riley leaned forward, curiosity piqued. "What kind of weird?" Jace filled him in on the story, from the envelope to the strange recording. Riley's smirk faded as he listened. When Biz finished, Riley stared at the tape with a frown.

"Trevor Langston?" he muttered. "Man, I thought they found his backpack in the woods or something. He's been gone a long time." Biz crossed his arms. "Yeah, but... what if he's not? Or at least—what if he wasn't gone when this was recorded?"

Riley scratched the back of his neck, deep in thought. "You think this has something to do with that station? 101.9?" - "We do," Jace said. "And we're thinking we need to go there."

The old radio station wasn't far—it sat just on the outskirts of town, near the edge of the woods. **The building had been abandoned for years**, and most kids avoided it, claiming it was haunted. They decided to head there that afternoon, fueled by the kind of reckless curiosity that only teenagers can muster. Riley grabbed his portable boombox, just in case, and they biked through the sleepy streets toward the station.

When they reached the crumbling structure, Biz felt a prickling sensation along the back of his neck. The station looked worse than he remembered—windows broken, graffiti scrawled across the walls, and the front door hanging off its hinges. It was the kind of place that shouldn't exist outside of nightmares. "Let's make this quick," Biz muttered, pushing his bike against the wall.

Inside, the air was stale and heavy, filled with the smell of mildew and old wiring. They crept through the darkened hallways, flashlights sweeping across faded posters and rusted equipment.

The deeper they went, the more Biz felt that strange sensation—**like the building was listening to them.**

At last, they found the old recording room. Most of the equipment was smashed or covered in dust, but the ancient radio console still sat in the corner, wires dangling like veins from a corpse.

Riley set the boombox on the table and switched it on. The speakers crackled, filling the room with a sea of static. Biz stepped closer to the console, heart pounding. Then, **he heard it**—just for a moment, buried beneath the static. A faint voice. Trevor's voice. The static hummed louder, buzzing like a swarm of angry bees. Biz leaned in, trying to make out the words, but the voice slipped away into the noise.

Suddenly, Riley jerked back from the boombox. "What the—?!" The boombox's speaker distorted violently, and the voice that came through wasn't Trevor's. It was low, deep, and inhuman—a whisper that felt like it crawled inside their heads. *"You shouldn't have come..."*

Biz's stomach twisted, and for a second, he swore the temperature in the room dropped ten degrees. Then—just as quickly as it began—the boombox cut out, leaving only silence. Jace stared at Biz, eyes wide. "Tell me that wasn't Trevor."

"It wasn't," Biz whispered, swallowing hard. "But I think it knew we were coming." The boys leave the station in a hurry, fear gnawing at them as they bike away. The mystery deepens—whatever they've stumbled into is far more dangerous than they realized. With new questions swirling in their heads and **something clearly watching their every move,** the investigation is only just beginning.

Chapter 3:

Biz sat slumped in his chair at the breakfast table, the boombox from the radio station still on the floor by his backpack. The events at the station churned in his mind, relentless and heavy like a storm about to break. He stirred his cereal absentmindedly, spoon clinking against the bowl.

The whisper from the static repeated in his head, looping: *"You shouldn't have come..."* He hadn't told his parents anything. **How could he?** They'd think he was losing it—or worse, tell him to stop seeing his friends. He knew this was something only **he, Jace, and Riley** could figure out.

Across the kitchen, the radio on the counter suddenly clicked on by itself. The old rock station was playing a crackling song—*Blue Öyster Cult's "(Don't Fear) The Reaper."* Biz stared at the radio, skin crawling.

The knobs turned on their own. **The volume dial twisted higher.** His heart raced. He scrambled toward it, yanking the power cord from the wall. The radio went silent instantly, leaving only the sound of his shallow breathing. This wasn't over.

That afternoon, Biz met Jace and Riley at **Sandy's Diner**, a small burger joint that smelled of grease and root beer. They slid into their usual booth, the jukebox at the end of the table humming softly.

Biz leaned forward, speaking low. "We need to figure this out. Whatever's happening, it's getting worse." Riley nodded, his face serious for once. "Yeah, no kidding. That voice back at the station—what the hell was that?" Jace picked at his fries, his usual grin replaced with a nervous twitch. "I say we go back—get more tapes if we can. Maybe there's more on them about Trevor."

"Are you nuts?" Riley hissed. "We barely got out of there the first time!" - "But we have to know," Biz insisted. "Trevor's trying to tell us something." Jace shrugged. "So... we go back at night, right?" Riley groaned. "Of course at night. Because *that's* not stupid at all. And who would we be without doing the stupid things we do?"

Later that evening, as the streetlights buzzed to life and shadows swallowed the town, the boys met by the edge of the woods behind the radio station. **The old building loomed dark and silent**, the windows glinting faintly beneath the rising moon.

Biz clutched a flashlight, sweat prickling his palms. The cool autumn wind whispered through the trees, carrying with it the faint scent of wet leaves and decay.

Jace shot them a grin, skateboard tucked under his arm. "Alright, Ghostbusters. Let's do this." They crept toward the broken entrance, the old door groaning as they eased it open. Inside, **the air was even heavier** than during the day, and the silence was thick enough to choke on.

The boys switched on their flashlights, beams cutting through the darkness. **The static hum they'd heard earlier was gone—but it felt as though something unseen was still here.** The walls seemed closer, pressing in around them, and the dim light flickered eerily off the shattered glass scattered across the floor.

They found the **old recording room** again, and Biz's heart raced when he saw it: another cassette tape, sitting perfectly in the center of the console, as if someone—or something—had left it there just for them.

Biz picked up the cassette with trembling fingers. The label read: **"PLAY ME. SIDE A."** He glanced at the others, and Jace gave him a nod. "We came this far. Might as well." Riley rolled his eyes but held out the boombox. "If this thing eats my batteries, I'm blaming you." They slid the tape into the player and hit **Play.** The hiss of static returned, and then—softly, like a whisper carried on the wind—they heard Trevor's voice again.

"The broadcast never ended..." Trevor's voice was faint, distorted, as if coming from the other side of a long tunnel. *"They thought shutting down the station would stop it... but they were wrong."*

The boys exchanged uneasy glances, the room growing colder with each passing second. Trevor's voice continued, urgent now: *"The DJ isn't what you think. He—"* Suddenly, the tape **warped**, the voice breaking into a sharp scream before the boombox cut off abruptly. They stood in stunned silence, the darkness pressing in around them. And then, **as if on que, they heard a sound**. A shuffling noise.

From **somewhere deeper in the station**, something dragged across the floor—slow and deliberate, as though it knew exactly where they were. Riley's flashlight beam wobbled. "We should leave. Like, *now*." Jace tilted his head, listening. "Wait... do you hear that?"

At first, Biz thought it was more static, but then he recognized it: the sound of a **song playing backward**, the warped melody twisting through the air. It seemed to come from everywhere and nowhere at once. And beneath it—something else. A voice. Low, garbled. Repeating the same phrase, over and over:

"Play it again... Play it again..." Jace's grin faltered. "Yeah, nope. I'm done."

They bolted for the exit, shoes pounding against the dusty floor. As they ran, the **backward song grew louder**, the eerie notes twisting in the air like smoke. They didn't stop until they were back outside, gasping for breath beneath the cold night sky.

Biz clutched the new tape tightly, heart hammering in his chest. **They weren't safe—not even outside.** The eerie song still rang in his ears, and the whispering voice seemed to cling to his skin like damp fog. "We need to figure out what's on this thing," Biz panted. "There's more to this, we're missing something." Jace nodded, wiping sweat from his brow. "That song—it was like... it was trying to get us to play the tape again." Riley shook his head. "You guys are insane. We need to smash that thing and forget this ever happened."

"We can't," Biz said, gripping the cassette tighter. "Trevor's in there. He's trying to tell us something. We just have to figure out what."

They regrouped in **Riley's basement**, the boombox perched on the coffee table. The room was dimly lit by a single lamp, casting long shadows across the walls. Biz slipped the new cassette into the player, his fingers trembling slightly. "Okay... one more time." The tape clicked into place, and the boys braced themselves as the hiss of static returned. This time, the message was clearer:

"The signal is trapped. The DJ is using it... He's still playing the final song. You have to stop it."

Biz felt a chill crawl down his spine. Trevor's voice continued: *"It's not just the radio. The Boathouse... it's all connected. They're waiting there. If you hear the song—"*

The tape cut off again, the final words swallowed by static. "The Boathouse?" Jace said, eyes wide. "That old concert venue?" Riley groaned. "You mean the place that's been shut down for, like, ten years? Great. That's exactly where I *don't* want to go."

Biz's heart raced. He knew—deep down—that this was the next step. Trevor's message was clear: something was happening at **The Boathouse**, and they had to stop it.

"We have to go," Biz whispered. "If the broadcast is still playing... if it's connected to the Boathouse..." Jace grinned, adrenaline lighting up his face. "Then we're going ghost hunting. Let's go Scooby-doo this place"

Chapter 4:

The Boathouse loomed in the distance like a forgotten relic, swallowed by shadows and strangled by vines. It sat at the edge of town, buried behind a line of skeletal trees whose branches tangled like grasping hands. The old concert venue had been closed for nearly a decade—long enough for **the town to forget it existed**, but not long enough for the walls to stop murmuring with secrets.

As Biz, Jace, and Riley approached on their bikes, the wind seemed to shift, carrying the faint smell of **stale beer and cigarette smoke**, as if the echoes of past concerts still clung to the air. **The front entrance was chained shut**, rusted links tangled across the doors like barbed wire, but the kids knew they wouldn't enter that way.

There was a hole in the fence at the back, hidden among the weeds. Jace had heard about it from **Kevin Larson**, a kid with a reputation for knowing the town's dark history.

"This place gives me the creeps," Riley muttered as they dropped their bikes in the overgrown grass. Jace grinned. "Good. That means we're on the right track."

Biz stared up at the **cracked marquee**, the letters faded and jumbled, but something about them sent a prickle of unease down his spine. The words seemed scrambled—like they formed a message only **the desperate could understand.** He shivered, rubbing the goosebumps on his arms. "Let's get this over with."

They wriggled through the torn fence and slipped inside the back entrance. **The hallway beyond was choked with dust** and smelled of mildew, the air thick and stale. The kids clicked on their flashlights, beams cutting jagged paths through the darkness. **Their footsteps echoed too loudly**, bouncing off the cracked walls and faded posters still clinging to the plaster.

Jace led the way, his skateboard tucked under his arm. "You know, people say this place is haunted. Back when it closed, a band was supposed to play the final show—but they never made it." - "Why?" Riley asked, his voice low. Jace smirked. "Some say they disappeared. Others say they *never left*." Biz shot Jace a warning glance. "Not helping."

They passed through the **lobby**, where old ticket stubs littered the floor like brittle leaves. **The air felt strange—thick with expectation**, as if the walls were holding their breath, waiting for something.

Then Biz saw **a flicker of movement.** Just at the edge of his vision—gone the second he turned his head. His flashlight beam swept across the room, but there was nothing there. His heart began to race. He knew—*deep down*—that they weren't alone.

The kids pushed open a pair of heavy doors and stepped into the **main auditorium.** The room was massive, the ceiling arching high above them, lost in shadows. Rows of empty seats stretched into the gloom, and at the far end of the room stood the **stage**—a ghostly skeleton of wood and metal, bathed in faint moonlight seeping through shattered windows.

Riley let out a low whistle. "Creepy doesn't even begin to cover it." Biz's eyes locked on the stage. Something about it felt... *wrong*. He imagined figures standing there, instruments in hand, waiting to play the final note of a song that never ended. Suddenly, **a sound echoed from the far end of the room.**

A single, discordant note—like someone strumming an out-of-tune guitar string. The kids froze. Jace whispered, "Did you hear that?" Biz nodded, his throat dry. They edged closer to the stage, each step dragging through the thick silence like walking through a dream. As they reached the foot of the stage, Biz noticed something: **an old cassette player** resting on a folding chair in the corner, the tape inside turning slowly. His heart dropped.

Without thinking, Biz reached out and stopped the tape. **The spinning wheels clicked to a halt, and the silence that followed felt heavier than before.** "That's... not creepy at all," Riley muttered, backing away from the stage. Then—just as suddenly—the **player clicked back on by itself.** The tape whirred to life, and **music filled the air**. But it wasn't any song Biz recognized—it was warped and broken, like a lullaby played through shattered glass.

And then, layered beneath the eerie tune, Biz heard it: *Trevor's voice.* It was faint, almost buried beneath the static, but unmistakable. *"They're here... The song never ended... Don't listen too long."*

The music warped again, twisting into strange, jarring notes, and Biz felt a sudden pressure in his skull—**like something was trying to crawl into his thoughts.** "Turn it off!" Jace shouted, panic rising in his voice.

Biz slammed his hand on the Stop button. **The music cut off instantly.** The kids stood frozen, hearts pounding, the silence pressing down on them once again. Before any of them could speak, Riley's flashlight beam wobbled and landed on

something odd—a small hatch, barely visible, set into the floor just behind the stage.

Jace crouched down, brushing away dust and debris to reveal the **trapdoor.** "Guess we found where they keep the bodies," Jace muttered with a nervous grin, trying to mask his fear. Biz swallowed hard. **Every instinct told him not to open it.** But he knew they had no choice. If Trevor's message was right—if everything was connected to this place—they had to see what was down there.

The old wood creaked as Jace pulled the trapdoor open. **A cold, stale breeze wafted from the darkness below**, carrying with it the faint scent of damp earth.

Riley peered into the opening. "There's a ladder. You first, Biz." Biz shot him a look but didn't argue. **Something was pulling him down there**—a strange compulsion, as if the answers were waiting just below the surface.

They climbed down into the **darkness**, their flashlights casting jittery beams along the crumbling walls. The basement was vast—**a labyrinth of old storage rooms and forgotten equipment**, the air thick with dust and shadows.

As they moved deeper into the space, the sound of **soft whispers** began to drift through the air. Biz couldn't tell if it was real or just in his mind, but the voices seemed to swirl around him—faint, fragmented words that hinted at things better left unknown. Then they found it something.

A wall covered in old posters and flyers. Most of them were faded beyond recognition, but one stood out—a **flyer for the final show at The Boathouse**, dated for 1979. The band's name was crossed out with red ink, and beneath it, scrawled in jagged letters, was a single sentence: **"The song never ends."**

A chill ran down Biz's spine. **He knew**—somehow—that they weren't alone in the basement. He turned, heart hammering in his chest, and his flashlight beam swept across the far wall.

For a moment, **he saw them**: shadowy figures standing perfectly still, just at the edge of the light. Their faces were twisted, featureless, **like wax melted beneath a flame.** Biz's breath caught in his throat.

The figures didn't move. They simply stood there, waiting, as if they had been waiting for a very long time. And then, in the faintest of whispers, **they spoke.** *"Play it again."*

Biz stumbled backward, heart slamming against his ribs. "We need to leave. Now." Jace didn't argue. Neither did Riley. They scrambled back toward the ladder, the whispers following them like shadows creeping through the cracks in the walls. The shadows jerked and twitched unnaturally.

Chapter 5:

The wind clawed at their faces as Biz, Jace, and Riley pedaled furiously through the night, hearts still racing from what they'd seen in The Boathouse's basement. **The eerie whisper—"Play it again"—echoed in Biz's head**, haunting every turn of the bike tires on the cracked pavement.

None of them spoke as they rode toward Riley's house. It was the kind of silence you didn't dare break—the kind that clung to you when you were trying to convince yourself that everything was fine, even though you knew deep down it wasn't.

When they finally reached Riley's driveway, they ditched their bikes and hurried inside, slamming the basement door behind them as if that could keep the dark out. For a long moment, **no one spoke**.

Riley flopped onto the couch, rubbing his eyes. "Okay, what the hell was that?" Jace sat cross-legged on the floor, chewing on the sleeve of his hoodie. "I told you this whole town is haunted. You guys never believe me."

Biz stood by the door, his arms crossed tightly over his chest, trying to stop the tremor running through him. "Those things... in the basement. They weren't... human." Riley let out a shaky laugh. "Yeah, no kidding. They looked like melted mannequins."

"But they spoke," Biz whispered. **"They said to play it again."** The words sent a shiver down his spine. He could still hear the whispers, cold and insistent, threading through his thoughts.

"What does that even mean?" Jace asked, rubbing the back of his neck. "What do they want us to play? The cassette?" Biz shook his head. "No. I think it's something bigger. I think… it's the song. The one Trevor warned us about. It's still playing—somehow." Riley groaned and pulled a blanket over his head. "Great. We're cursed. This is how it starts. Pretty soon we'll all be puking up black stuff and screaming backwards."

"Dude, stop," Jace muttered, shooting him a look. Biz paced the room, his mind racing. "There has to be a way to stop it. Trevor's trying to tell us something—he keeps talking about the DJ. And the broadcast."

Jace perked up. "Right—101.9 FM. What if we tune in? Maybe the broadcast is still out there." Riley dragged his old **shortwave radio** out from under the couch, grumbling the whole time. "If this thing blows up or summons a demon, I'm blaming you two."

Biz sat cross-legged on the floor, twisting the dial slowly, searching for **the signal.** The radio hissed and crackled with bursts of static as they flipped through frequencies, the room thick with tension. And then—it happened. **The needle hit 101.9 FM.**

The static cleared, and **a low hum filled the room**, vibrating through their bones. It wasn't music—it was a single note, stretched long and low, like a warning siren from a distant world.

Then came **the voice.** It was soft at first, just a whisper beneath the hum. But as Biz leaned closer, the voice grew louder, more distinct:

"...The final song... Play it to the end... Bring them back..." Biz's heart thudded against his ribs. He knew that voice. **It was Trevor.** The radio hissed again, and Trevor's voice became frantic: *"Don't let it finish! You have to stop it before—"*

The broadcast cut off abruptly, replaced by a high-pitched **screech** that made the boys wince and cover their ears. The radio fizzled out completely, leaving only silence in its wake. For a moment, none of them moved. **The silence felt alive, pressing in from all sides, cold and suffocating.** And then—without remorse, it began.

The lights flickered. The basement walls seemed to **breathe,** expanding and contracting with a strange, rhythmic pulse. The air turned bitterly cold, and Biz felt the hair on the back of his neck stand on end. From the corner of the room, **something shifted.**

The shadows—deep and inky—peeled away from the walls, pooling together into a twisted shape. **A figure emerged,** tall and skeletal, with limbs too long and joints that bent the wrong way.

Its face—or what was left of it—was smooth and blank, like a melted mask. And as it stepped forward, **its body crackled like old vinyl,** distorting and glitching in and out of existence. The boys froze, paralyzed by fear.

The thing tilted its head, and from somewhere deep within its warped form, **a whisper escaped:** *"Play it again..."* Jace was the first to react. "RUN!"

They bolted for the stairs, shoes pounding against the floor. The creature moved after them, limbs jerking in unnatural spasms, its distorted form **flickering** in and out of the shadows.

They reached the top of the stairs just as **the basement lights exploded**, plunging everything into darkness. Biz slammed the door shut, heart racing, and twisted the lock. They stood there, gasping for breath, the cold sweat clinging to their skin. "Tell me that didn't just happen," Riley whispered, his voice shaking. "It happened," Biz panted, pressing his back against the door. "It's real."

The three boys huddled together in the hallway, the silence around them thick and suffocating. **The thing in the basement wasn't gone**—they could feel it waiting just behind the door, patient and hungry.

"We need to stop the song," Biz whispered, wiping sweat from his brow. "Whatever's playing—it's what's bringing them back."

"How?" Riley asked, still clutching the shortwave radio like a lifeline. "What the hell do we do?" Biz thought for a moment, heart thudding against his ribs. And then he remembered something—**the trapdoor in The Boathouse.**

"The broadcast," he said suddenly. "It's connected to The Boathouse. That's where we have to go. We need to find the source—destroy whatever's keeping the song going." Jace stared at him, wide-eyed. "You're saying we need to go back there?" Biz nodded grimly. "It's the only way." Riley groaned. "Of course it is. Because every dumb horror movie ever made starts exactly like this."

They agreed to meet the next night, just after sunset. **The Boathouse was their only lead**, and if Trevor's warnings were true, they were running out of time. Before they left, Biz made one last decision. He picked up the cassette—the one they'd found on the stage—and slipped it into his jacket pocket.

He had a feeling they were going to need it.

Chapter 6:

The next night came swiftly, dragging a cold wind behind it. **The sky was bruised and swollen with clouds**, casting a dim, washed-out glow over the town. Biz, Jace, and Riley met at their usual spot—Riley's driveway—each of them carrying the weight of what was to come.

None of them had slept much since the encounter with the shadowy figure in the basement. The feeling that **something was following them** lingered, like a stain they couldn't wash away. Every creak, every flicker of light, felt like the edges of the world fraying around them. And now, they were going back to **The Boathouse**—to find whatever waited beneath it. Jace tightened the straps on his backpack. "You guys ready for this?"

"No," Riley muttered. "But here we are." Biz zipped his jacket, feeling the reassuring weight of the **cassette tape** in his pocket. "Let's end this." The boys pedaled through the empty streets, the wind biting at their faces. When they reached The Boathouse, the old venue looked even worse than before—**the windows like black eyes**, staring blankly into the night.

"Last chance to bail," Riley whispered as they propped their bikes against the side wall. Jace grinned nervously. "Where's the fun in that?"

They slipped through the torn fence, the weeds hissing underfoot like warning whispers. **The back entrance gaped**

open, waiting for them. They clicked on their flashlights and stepped inside.

The air inside The Boathouse was colder than before, as if the building knew why they had returned. **Every step echoed strangely**, the sound folding back on itself, making the boys feel like they were walking through someone else's memory.

When they reached the **trapdoor** at the edge of the stage, Biz hesitated, heart thudding in his chest. **Whatever was down there, it wanted them to come.** "Let's just get this over with," Riley muttered, flicking his flashlight nervously.

They opened the trapdoor, the hinges groaning in protest. **A blast of cold air greeted them**, carrying with it the faintest sound of music—**warped notes drifting through the darkness** like a lullaby sung by something long dead.

One by one, they climbed down the ladder, flashlights bobbing in the dark. The walls of the basement seemed to close in around them, the shadows thicker and **more oppressive** than before. **The air was heavy with static**, crackling faintly against their skin.

They reached the bottom and found themselves standing in **a large underground chamber**. The walls were lined with old speakers and tangled wires, and at the center of the room stood **a massive reel-to-reel recorder**, the tape spinning slowly, endlessly.

Biz's breath hitched in his throat. **This was it**—the heart of the broadcast. The machine that had been playing the cursed song for decades. Jace stepped closer, flashlight beam flickering across the ancient equipment. "Is that... what I think it is?" Biz nodded. **"The Final Broadcast."** The reel-to-reel player had been running all these years, looping the song in endless cycles, feeding it into the airwaves—keeping the curse alive.

Riley stared at the spinning tape, a deep unease settling over him. "If we stop it... what happens?" - "We find out," Biz whispered, stepping toward the machine. He reached out, hand trembling, and pressed **Stop.**

The machine whirred, the tape stuttering to a halt. For a moment, **everything went silent**—a deep, unnatural silence that pressed against their ears, making it hard to breathe. And then, from the shadows, **a voice spoke.** *"You shouldn't have stopped it."*

The boys whirled around, flashlights shaking in their hands. **The shadows peeled away from the far wall**, revealing a figure standing there—tall and thin, with limbs too long and joints that bent the wrong way. Its face was a smooth mask, featureless and terrible. *The DJ.*

Biz's heart pounded in his chest. He could feel **the weight of the cassette tape in his pocket**, pulsing like a heartbeat. Somehow, he knew that this was the thing Trevor had warned them about—the DJ who had kept the song playing, keeping the curse alive. "Play it again," the DJ whispered, its voice a low, crackling hiss. "Play it to the end."

The shadows around it swirled, flickering like flames in the wind. **The room grew colder**, the air thick with static and the hum of unseen frequencies. "We're not playing anything," Jace muttered, gripping his flashlight tighter. The DJ tilted its head, as if amused. "You don't have a choice."

Biz's hand shot into his pocket, fingers closing around the **cassette tape**. He pulled it out, heart racing, and shoved it into the portable boombox Riley carried. "What are you doing?" Riley hissed, panic in his voice.

Biz's hands trembled as he pressed **Play**. **The cassette whirred to life**, the wheels turning slowly—and then the music began. It was the same warped, broken melody they had heard before, twisting through the air like smoke. But this time, beneath the music, Biz heard something else: **Trevor's voice.** *"You're almost there... Just a little longer..."*

The DJ hissed, its body flickering like a damaged film reel. "Stop it," it whispered, voice crackling. "Stop the tape." But Biz didn't stop. **He knew**—somehow—that Trevor was guiding them, that they were close to ending the curse once and for all.

The music grew louder, filling the room with discordant notes and static. The DJ snarled, its body unraveling, shadows twisting and writhing around it like serpents.

"Now!" Biz shouted. "Destroy the machine!" Jace didn't hesitate. **He grabbed a rusted pipe from the floor** and swung it at the reel-to-reel player with all his strength. **The machine exploded in a shower of sparks and shattered metal**, the tape unraveling like a snake's skin.

The moment the machine broke, **the DJ let out a terrible, inhuman scream**—a sound that vibrated through the walls and rattled their bones. Its body flickered violently, glitching in and out of existence.

Biz hit **Stop** on the cassette player. **The music cut off instantly.** And with it, **the DJ busts into twisted lengths of tape like an old, busted cassette and dissolved into the shadows**, its form collapsing into a swirl of black mist that dissipated into the cold air. The boys stood in stunned silence, hearts pounding in their chests. **The room was still.** It was over.

The boys climbed back up the ladder, their bodies aching with exhaustion but **relieved** beyond words. The air outside felt fresh and alive, the cold wind no longer carrying the scent of stale smoke and static.

Jace let out a breathless laugh. "We actually did it." Riley slumped against the wall, wiping sweat from his brow. "I'm never going into another haunted building again. Ever." Biz pulled the cassette tape from the boombox and stared at it. **Trevor's voice was silent now**, but somehow, he knew his friend was finally at peace.

They stood there for a moment, the weight of everything settling over them. **The curse was broken.** The song had ended. For the first time in a long while, **the night felt quiet.**

Chapter 7:

The cool night folded around them like a dark ocean, thick with the scent of rusted metal and old rain. A strange stillness clung to the walls of The Boathouse, as though the building had finally exhaled after years of holding its breath. But something deeper stirred beneath that quiet—**the kind of silence that comes when a song isn't finished but merely paused, waiting for the needle to drop once more.**

The boys stood at the edge of the wrecked reel-to-reel player, the tangled ribbons of cassette tape curled at their feet like dead snakes. The shadows had settled into a peculiar kind of calm, no longer flickering or bending toward them as they had moments before. But **still**, Biz could feel it—something left behind, a presence too stubborn to fully leave.

Jace wiped a grimy hand across his face, glancing at the broken machine. "Is it really over?" he whispered, almost afraid of his own words, like the act of speaking might awaken whatever lay dormant in the wreckage.

Riley leaned heavily against the wall, clutching his knees. "It better be. I don't think my heart can take much more of this."

Biz stood apart from them, gripping the battered cassette in his hand. His pulse beat against the plastic like a second heartbeat, each thrum a whisper that the night was not as empty as it seemed. **The weight in his chest had shifted, but not**

entirely gone. Something unfinished still threaded itself through the air, like a melody left unresolved.

He slipped the cassette into his pocket, and the cold pressed deeper against his ribs, as if the tape itself was unwilling to be forgotten.

They slipped through the back fence, bikes waiting where they had left them, wheels slick with dew. No one spoke as they pedaled into the waiting arms of the night. **The streets stretched out before them, dark and restless, the hum of distant streetlights buzzing low in their ears.**

Biz kept his eyes on the road, watching the way the moonlight pooled in puddles along the asphalt, staining the world with pale silver. Each turn of the wheels seemed to drag against him, the air heavy with expectation, as though the night itself was reluctant to let them go.

The houses leaned toward them, windows glinting in the dim, like they were **watching**. Biz imagined figures standing behind those glass panes—faces half-forgotten, flickering in and out of view, waiting for the boys to pass before fading back into the dark.

He tightened his grip on the handlebars. **Something was following them**—not in the way that things with feet or wheels follow, but in the way that memories linger, clinging to skin like the scent of smoke.

They reached Riley's house and dropped their bikes in the driveway, the metal clattering too loud against the quiet. Inside, the basement lights flickered overhead, buzzing with a static that didn't belong. Riley muttered a curse and gave the nearest lamp a frustrated tap, but it didn't stop the flicker—it was as if the lights were breathing in time with something just out of reach.

Biz set the cassette player down on the coffee table, the weight of it making the wood groan beneath its age. He stared at it, **the silence between them thickening like fog, curling with every unspoken word.** It was supposed to be over, but the feeling in his chest told him otherwise.

There, in the hum of the failing lights and the slow creak of old wood, **a whisper gathered itself**—soft at first, like a breeze stirring the edges of a forgotten memory. Riley froze, his eyes locked on the cassette player. "You hear that?" **The sound curled from the speakers, Trevor's voice, distant, warped, but unmistakably there.** *"You need to rewind it... just one more time."*

Biz's stomach twisted as the words crawled into his mind. There was a pull inside him, something deep and wrong, like an itch buried too far beneath the skin to scratch. **He knew—somehow—that the tape wasn't finished, that it needed one more spin through the machine.** But that realization carried with it a weight, a truth heavier than the walls pressing in around them.

"We're not playing it again," Riley whispered, voice sharp with fear. "We destroyed the machine. We're done. It's over." Biz's hand trembled as he reached for the cassette. "What if we're wrong?" Jace shook his head, backing away from the table. "Dude. Don't. We made it out. Don't mess with this."

But Biz knew, in the pit of his stomach, that they hadn't truly escaped. **The song was still there, unfinished, hanging in the air like a thread waiting to be pulled.** And something—whatever haunted the edges of their world—would not leave until it played to the end.

With shaking fingers, Biz slid the tape into the player. **The machine whirred softly, the spools turning with a deliberate, steady click.** He pressed the rewind button.

The tape spun backward, the sound of music unraveling in slow, eerie fragments. **Melodies folded in on themselves, notes twisting into strange and unsettling shapes**, as if the song was being peeled away layer by layer, revealing something hidden beneath the surface. And then—**a voice, buried in the static.** It wasn't Trevor this time. It was someone else, **low and familiar,** the sound of it wrapping around Biz like cold hands in the dark. *"You're too late."*

The room shuddered. The walls seemed to ripple like water disturbed by a stone, and the air thickened with the scent of damp earth. **A shadow flickered at the edge of the room**, a shape coalescing out of the dark—a figure half-formed, flickering like a dying radio signal. Biz's breath hitched. He knew that shape, that looming presence. **The DJ had returned.**

The room buckled under the weight of the thing's presence. **The DJ stood at the edge of the light, its smooth, featureless face turned toward the boys with a kind of eerie patience.** It was not angry. It did not rage or scream. It only waited—because it knew what they did not: The song was never meant to end.

Biz's heart pounded, and in the pit of his soul, he knew the truth—the broadcast had only paused, waiting for the right moment to begin again. **And they had just given it that moment.**

The DJ raised one long, spindly hand, pointing toward the cassette player with a slow, deliberate motion. *"Play it again,"* it whispered, the words scraping against the edges of reality like nails on glass.

Biz's hands shook as the cassette clicked to a halt, the tape fully rewound. The weight of the DJ's command settled over him, **dragging him down into a darkness deeper than the night outside.** He knew what the voice wanted—what it had always wanted. **It needed them to finish the song.**

Jace's voice cracked as he spoke. "Don't. Whatever you do, don't press play." But the world seemed to narrow around Biz, the edges of his vision blurring until there was nothing left but the cassette player and the waiting shadow of the DJ. **The pull was irresistible**, like gravity, dragging him toward the button with a force too strong to fight.

He could feel it—**the tape was alive**, pulsing with the memory of every lost soul it carried, whispering promises of answers, of endings. But there were no endings here. Only loops. Only echoes. And before he could stop himself, **his thumb pressed down.**

The cassette clicked to life. **The song unfurled in the air, strange and beautiful, terrible and haunting.** It was a melody that did not belong in this world—**a song from somewhere else**, where time ran in circles and endings were only beginnings in disguise.

The DJ stepped forward, and the boys felt the room shift around them, the walls bending inward like the closing pages of a book. **The air hummed with the final note**, the sound sharp and sweet, twisting through their minds with the weight of something ancient and inevitable. And then—**it stopped.**

The silence that followed was heavier than anything they had ever known. **It pressed down on their chests**, filled their lungs, and for a moment, it felt as though the world had ended. But it hadn't.

The DJ smiled—a terrible, empty thing—and stepped backward into the shadows, dissolving into the darkness like smoke. **The song was over.**

And the world was left to pick up the pieces.

Chapter 8:

The night weighed heavy as the boys pedaled through empty streets, the cold biting deeper than before. Biz kept his head low, the handlebars vibrating beneath his grip. He could feel it—**the loop hadn't truly ended.** No matter how fast they pedaled, no matter how far they rode from it, **the song followed them**. Not in the air, not on the wind, but inside them—woven into their bones, waiting.

The lights flickered as they passed beneath streetlamps, brief bursts of static hissing in the cold air. Biz's heartbeat pounded in his ears, out of sync with the rhythm of the world. Even the night seemed warped—too still, as if **the town had been paused mid-dream.**

Jace skidded to a stop at an intersection, his breath clouding the air. "This... this doesn't feel right," he muttered, glancing down each empty street. **"It's like we never left."**

Riley coasted beside him, gripping the handlebars so tight his knuckles paled. "Maybe we didn't." Biz swallowed hard, the cassette still weighing heavy in his jacket pocket. He knew Riley wasn't joking.

When Biz finally stumbled through the door of his house, the hallway light flickered—**an electric pulse in perfect time with the song that lingered in his mind.** He dropped his bike by the door and stood there, frozen, waiting for something to shift—**for the walls to ripple, for the shadows to stretch toward him.**

Nothing happened. But the stillness felt wrong, like **an unfinished sentence waiting to be spoken.** His parents were already asleep upstairs, the faint hum of the television drifting down the hall. The house felt fragile, as though it existed only on the surface of something much deeper.

He reached into his jacket and pulled out the cassette, staring at the smooth, black plastic. The label—**SIDE A**—gleamed in the low light. He knew better than to play it again, but that didn't stop the urge from slithering into his mind. *One more time,* the thought whispered. *Just to be sure.*

Biz shoved the tape into the back of his desk drawer, slamming it shut. But even with it out of sight, **the song remained.** It hummed beneath his thoughts, like a second pulse—alive, waiting.

The night dragged on, slow and relentless. Biz lay in bed, staring at the ceiling, his mind heavy with exhaustion but too wired to sleep. Every time he closed his eyes, **he saw flickers of the DJ's face**—that smooth, featureless mask, bending and glitching at the edges of his vision.

And then there were the whispers—**soft, rhythmic murmurs** that crawled beneath his skin, threading through his veins like static. He knew they weren't real, but they felt real, and that was enough to keep him awake.

At some point, the walls seemed to shift—just slightly, like the room had shifted on its axis, tilting toward somewhere darker. The shadows stretched long and thin, and for a brief, horrible moment, **Biz thought he saw something standing at**

the foot of his bed. A figure. Silent. Waiting. He blinked—and it was gone. But the fear stayed, clinging to him like a cold sweat.

Biz woke to a pale, watery sunrise leaking through the blinds, though it offered no comfort. The house still felt **too quiet, like it was waiting for something to happen.** The cassette sat heavy in his desk drawer, **pulling at him even in its silence.**

Jace called just after noon, his voice strained and uneven. "You feel it too, right?" he asked, skipping past small talk. **"Like we're still stuck. Like it's not over."** Biz nodded, though Jace couldn't see him. "Yeah," he whispered. "It's not over."

"I've been hearing things, man," Jace admitted, his voice a low rasp. "Music. In my dreams. And when I wake up... it's still there." Riley joined them at Biz's house a few hours later, his face pale and drawn. "We broke the machine," he said, pacing the room. **"We stopped the broadcast. So why does it still feel like it's playing?"**

Biz didn't have an answer. But he knew one thing for sure: **The song hadn't ended. It had just changed.** They gathered in the basement, the heavy air pressing against their skin like a second layer of clothing. **The shortwave radio sat on the table, silent and waiting.** Jace flipped it on without a word, twisting the dial slowly, searching for a signal.

The static hissed, sharp and relentless, filling the room with a low, grating hum. And then—**beneath the noise—something stirred.** A song. Warped and distant, **the melody cracked at the edges**, as though it had been stretched too far across time. But the boys knew it instantly—it was **the song from the broadcast.**

Biz's heart raced. **The loop was still alive, playing somewhere out there in the static, waiting to pull them back in.** Jace leaned closer to the radio, his breath shallow. "It's still out there," he whispered, a mixture of awe and fear in his voice. "How?" Biz didn't answer. **He knew there were no answers—only more questions.**

As the song played, **a voice emerged from the static.** It was Trevor's voice again—faint and distorted, but unmistakable. *"You were never meant to stop it..."* Trevor whispered, his words unraveling like threads from a fraying rope. *"It doesn't end. It only rewinds."*

The boys stared at the radio, hearts pounding. **The signal twisted through the air**, filling the basement with strange, warping echoes. *"They'll come for you,"* Trevor's voice warned. *"Unless you finish the song..."*

The radio popped and fizzled, cutting off abruptly, leaving only silence. Riley stumbled back, hands trembling. "We broke it. We ended it. We—"

"We didn't end anything," Biz whispered. **The truth weighed heavy on his chest, cold and suffocating.** They had only scratched the surface—**the loop was deeper than they'd imagined.**

They sat in heavy silence, the weight of the song pressing against them, **pulling at their thoughts like threads unraveling from a spool.** Biz knew they had two choices: **they could run and hope the song wouldn't follow, or they could finish what they started.** But deep down, he knew there was only one real option.

"We have to go back," Biz whispered, his voice barely audible. "We have to finish it." Riley groaned, burying his head in his hands. "You're kidding me. Right? Please tell me you're kidding."

Jace gave a nervous laugh, though there was no joy in it. "Ghosts, curses, looped songs... this is officially the dumbest idea we've ever had." Biz stared at the radio, the cassette tape cold in his hand. **The song had trapped them—and the only way out was through.** "We end it," he said, more to himself than to the others. "For real this time."

Chapter 9:

The sky above them churned, a low, oppressive gray that pressed down like a hand on the back of their necks. **The cold wind scraped across their skin, heavy with the scent of wet stone and static.** The boys rode in silence, their bikes rattling over cracked pavement as the world folded inward, narrowing to the same twisted sense of inevitability that haunted their every step.

Biz kept the cassette in his pocket, the weight of it pulling at him, deeper with every breath. **The melody of the cursed song hummed in his mind**, not loud, but persistent—a quiet presence at the back of his thoughts, waiting to bloom into something terrible.

They had to go back. **They knew now that the song wasn't just music.** It was something alive—something that had clawed its way through the broadcast and latched onto the town, burrowing into the cracks of reality like a parasite.

Jace pedaled alongside him, his jaw tight, fingers clenched white-knuckled around the handlebars. "Are we really doing this, man?" he asked, though his voice lacked conviction—as if he already knew the answer.

Biz nodded, eyes fixed on the path ahead. "Yeah. We finish it." **The Boathouse waited for them**, dark and yawning at the edge of town, like the mouth of a slumbering beast that had only begun to stir.

The boys slipped through the hole in the fence, the tangled weeds brushing against their legs like cold fingers. **The Boathouse loomed above them**, a crumbling shell of rusted metal and cracked plaster. The windows were black, empty sockets that seemed to watch their every move.

They stepped through the back entrance, the door creaking on its hinges. **The air inside was thicker than before**, clinging to their skin like damp wool. Every sound—every breath, every footstep—was swallowed by the shadows, as if the building itself was absorbing them.

This time, there was no hesitating. **The trapdoor behind the stage waited, gaping open** like a wound that had never healed. They descended the ladder one by one, hearts thudding in their chests, the cold biting deeper the further they climbed.

When they reached the bottom, **the reel-to-reel machine sat in ruins**, just as they had left it. The tangled tape spilled across the floor like veins, unmoving, lifeless. But the room still thrummed with that same strange energy, humming in the walls, vibrating beneath their feet.

"It's still here," Riley whispered, his breath visible in the cold air. "I can feel it." Jace nodded grimly. "We didn't stop it... we just paused it."

Biz pulled the cassette from his jacket pocket. **The plastic felt too heavy—like it carried more than sound inside.** He knew what he had to do. But doing it felt like stepping off the edge of a cliff, knowing the fall would last forever.

He slipped the tape into the old boombox, his hands steady despite the knot of fear twisting in his gut. **The spools began to spin**, the machine clicking and whirring with mechanical precision.

The song drifted through the room, slow and warped, **notes folding in on themselves like a hymn sung underwater.** It was beautiful in a way that hurt—aching and jagged, a melody that promised both longing and loss. And beneath the music, **the whispers began.**

Biz recognized the voice. Trevor. His old friend, speaking through the static, his words a lifeline stretched across the void. *"You're almost there... just keep going..."*

The DJ's shadow began to gather in the corner of the room, **flickering in and out of focus, a glitch in the fabric of the world.** Its presence twisted the air, bending reality around it like the pull of a black hole. But Biz didn't stop the tape. **He knew—deep down—that this was the only way out.**

The song swelled, growing louder, **a crescendo that twisted through time, unraveling the loop that had held them prisoner.** The DJ moved closer, its featureless face tilting toward them, as if curious—watching, waiting. And then, **the song reached its final note.**

The world shuddered. **The walls cracked and folded inward, the ceiling dissolving into black mist.** The boys felt the ground shift beneath their feet, as if the floor had given way and they were falling—not into darkness, but into memory.

Time unraveled around them, peeling back in ribbons, revealing the fragments of every moment the broadcast had stolen. The missing kids, the final broadcast, Trevor's voice—**all of it woven into the same endless loop, spinning forever.**

For a moment, they saw it all—the ghosts trapped between frequencies, **their faces twisted with longing, desperate to be heard.** And then, like a radio being tuned to the right station, everything snapped into focus.

Biz felt the song reach its end—**a perfect, haunting silence that hummed with finality.** The DJ dissolved, its form scattering into the ether like ash on the wind. **The loop had been broken.**

The room settled, the air shifting back to something real—solid. **The reel-to-reel machine lay shattered on the floor, unmoving, its purpose finally fulfilled.** The boys stood in silence, hearts pounding, their breath coming in sharp bursts.

"It's over," Biz whispered, though the words felt strange on his tongue—**as if the truth was just slightly out of reach.** Jace let out a shaky laugh, rubbing his face with both hands. "We did it. We actually did it." Riley gave a nervous chuckle, though his eyes were still wide with disbelief. "Please tell me I'm not dreaming."

"You're not," Biz said, though even as he spoke, **he could still feel the faint hum of the song—just a memory now, lingering at the edges of his thoughts.**

They climbed back up the ladder, the cold night waiting for them outside. **The wind felt cleaner, lighter, as if something heavy had finally lifted.** For the first time in what felt like forever, the air didn't hum with static. And yet... **something lingered.** An echo, faint and distant, barely audible but still there—**the shadow of a song that had once held them captive.**

The boys rode home under the dim glow of the streetlights, their bikes rattling over the familiar streets. **The town felt the same, yet different**—as though the edges of reality had shifted just slightly, leaving behind a faint scar where the loop had once been.

Biz's thoughts drifted as they pedaled through the quiet night. **The song was over, but its memory remained—woven** into them, like a scar that wouldn't fully heal. They had broken free, but something told him that they would never truly be free of it.

At his doorstep, Biz turned to his friends. **Jace gave him a tired grin**, and Riley offered a lazy wave before they rode off into the night. Biz watched them disappear into the shadows, the hum of their bikes fading into silence. **The night closed in around him**, soft and still—just the way it had always been. But as he turned toward the door, he felt it—**the faintest pull, deep in his chest, like the last note of a song that refused to end.**

He slipped the cassette from his pocket one last time. The label gleamed in the moonlight—**SIDE A, waiting to be played again.** And in the silence that followed, **Biz thought he heard the faintest whisper.** *"Play it again..."*

Chapter 10:

The sun broke over the horizon, but **the light felt pale and thin**, barely warming the edges of the world. For the first time in weeks, the town seemed calm—**too calm**, like a picture painted over a deeper, darker truth.

Biz sat at the edge of his bed, the **cassette player resting silently on his desk**. His fingers itched to touch it, to feel the weight of it again, to press play and hear what still hummed beneath the surface. The song had ended—he knew it had. But its echo persisted, lingering in the cracks of his mind, as if **the music had sunk too deeply to be erased.**

He heard footsteps outside his window—**familiar voices**. Riley and Jace had come to check on him. Biz slipped the tape into his jacket pocket without thinking, the cool plastic pressing against his ribs like **a secret he couldn't bear to leave behind.**

In the crisp morning air, the boys sat huddled on Biz's front steps, their breath curling like smoke in the cold. **They looked like kids again**, but Biz knew better. They had seen too much. **There was no going back** to what they'd been before.

"So, that's it, right?" Riley asked, glancing nervously toward the street as if something might emerge from the shadows at any moment. "We're done?"

"Yeah," Jace muttered, though his tone carried no conviction. He stared at the pavement as if he could see the cracks spreading beneath it, deeper than they should go. "It's over." But it wasn't. **They all knew it.**

Biz exhaled slowly, the cassette's weight pressing heavy against his side. **The song had ended, but the silence it left behind felt like a promise waiting to be fulfilled.** Something unfinished. Something that whispered to him from just beyond reach.

Riley shifted uncomfortably, rubbing his hands together. "I keep thinking I'm gonna hear it again," he confessed quietly. "Like, out of nowhere… it's just gonna start playing." Jace shot Biz a look—one of those quick glances that carried a thousand unspoken fears. "It's not really over, is it?" he asked, his voice barely above a whisper. Biz shook his head. **He didn't have the heart to lie.**

That night, the dream came. Biz found himself standing **inside The Boathouse**, the walls yawning with static. The air was thick with electricity, humming through his veins, pulling at his mind like invisible threads. **He could hear the song—faint and far away—looping endlessly through the dark.** And there, at the edge of the stage, stood **the DJ.**

Its featureless face tilted toward Biz, waiting patiently, like it had always known this moment would come. **The shadows around it flickered, alive and restless,** twisting into shapes that teased at recognition.

The DJ reached out, **one long finger pointing directly at Biz's jacket.** Biz's hand moved of its own accord, slipping into his pocket, pulling out the cassette. **It gleamed in the pale light—waiting, always waiting.** "You know what to do," the DJ whispered, its voice crawling into Biz's mind like static. "It never ends."

Biz sat bolt upright in bed, **his heart hammering in his chest.** The dream clung to him, heavy as wet clothes, the DJ's whisper still rattling through his thoughts. **The cassette was cold against his ribs**, pressing against him like a reminder.

He knew what the DJ had meant—**the loop wasn't broken. It had only begun again.** The silence around him felt too perfect, as if the air itself was waiting for the next note. **Somewhere, out there in the night, the song still hummed—quiet, patient, inevitable.** And he knew—**deep down—there was no stopping it.**

The next morning, Biz met Jace and Riley by the skate park, **the air heavy with unspoken dread.** They sat on the concrete ramp, their bikes lying in the grass, and watched the world go about its business—kids laughing, cars passing, life moving forward as if nothing had changed. But the boys knew better. **They carried the truth like a splinter lodged deep in their minds.**

"We have to do something," Biz whispered, breaking the silence. "It's not over." Riley groaned. "You've got to be kidding me." Jace stared at Biz, his expression a mix of exhaustion and fear. "What are you saying, man? We destroyed the machine. We finished the song."

Biz shook his head slowly, the weight of the truth settling in his chest. "It's not about the machine," he said softly. "It's about the loop. **It's always going to play, no matter what we do.**" The silence that followed felt like the final note of a song, hanging in the air, refusing to fade.

That night, they gathered in Riley's basement for what they knew would be their final act. **The cassette player sat on the coffee table**, silent and waiting. The cassette gleamed in Biz's hand—small, unassuming, but heavy with the weight of everything it carried. "We finish it," Biz whispered. "For real this time."

Jace swallowed hard, his face pale. "And if it doesn't work?" Biz met his gaze, the fear etched deep in his bones. "Then we're stuck with it. Forever." The words hung in the air, heavy and absolute. **There was no going back.** Biz slid the cassette into the player, his hands steady. **The tape whirred to life, the spools turning slowly, deliberately.**

The song drifted through the room—soft, warped, and beautiful, a melody that pulled at the edges of their souls. **It was a lullaby from the end of the world**, and it carried the weight of every moment the boys had lived and lost. As the final note approached, **the air shimmered**, bending around them like light through water. The DJ's voice whispered from the static: *"Play it again... or it never ends."*

The boys exchanged a glance—**the kind of look shared between those who have seen too much, who have walked through the dark and come out changed.** And then—**the song ended.**

For a long moment, the world was silent. **Perfectly, beautifully silent.** The boys sat in the basement, hearts pounding, waiting for the air to shift, for the loop to pull them back in. But the silence held—**not the waiting silence of unfinished business, but the kind that comes when something has truly ended.**

Biz exhaled slowly, the weight in his chest lifting for the first time in what felt like forever. **It was over.** Riley let out a breathless laugh, wiping his face with both hands. "Did we actually do it this time?"

Jace grinned, though exhaustion pulled at the corners of his mouth. "Yeah... I think we did." Biz stared at the cassette player, his mind oddly quiet—**no song, no whispers, just the sound of the world moving forward.** And for the first time, **he believed it.**

The boys rode through the quiet streets, **the wind in their hair, the stars spread out above them like promises.** The night no longer hummed with static, no longer pulled at the edges of their thoughts. They had broken free.

As Biz reached his house, **he pulled the cassette from his pocket one last time.** It felt light now—just a piece of plastic, nothing more.

He smiled and, without hesitation, tossed it into the trash. **The loop was broken.** And this time, it would stay that way.

Also by B. Humphrey

Bigfoot Vs
Bigfoot Vs Werewolves
Bigfoot Vs Vampires
Bigfoot Vs Aliens
Bigfoot Vs Yeti
Bigfoot Vs Werebear
Bigfoot Vs Mothman
Bigfoot Vs The Kandahar Giant
Bigfoot Vs Chimera
Bigfoot Vs Loch Ness Monster
Bigfoot Vs Wendigo
The Great Cryptid Wars
The Moon Curse Saga
Bigfoot Vs: The Collector's Edition Books 1-10

Retro Horrors: The Lost Decade
Cassette Ghosts
Summer of the Black Star
The Arcade Incident

Dead End Drive – In
The Polaroid Project
Endless Paths: The Choose-Your-Own Doom Chronicles
Neon Dreams
The Forgotten Carnival
Satanic Panic
Skin of the Moon

The Autumn Folklore Chronicles
The Forest Of Forgotten Names
The Witch Of Windspindle Hollow
The Burrowfolk Chronicles

The Fall Of America
The Final Directive

The Phantom Finders Club
A Haunting On Maplewood Street
The Secrets Of Old Fort Tower
Ghosts OF The Infirmary

The Saturn Outlaws
The Saturn Outlaws: Sky-Bandits of the Void Frontier

The Starling Sleuths
Detective Starling vol. 1
Detective Starling Vol. 2

Winter Horrors
Whispers of the Wendigo
Cold Cuts
The Dark Beneath

Standalone
The Witch of Blackwood Hollow
The Storied Mind
The Great Cryptid Wars
Sporefall
Chronicles of the Hairy Kind: A Field Log by Thaddeus Grieve